The Bat Conspiracy.
The Beginning.

By

Solange Wojnowski

Copyright ©2022 Solange Wojnowski

All rights reserved.

"The Bat Conspiracy. The Beginning" published through Young Author Academy.

Young Author Academy FZCO

Dubai, United Arab Emirates

www.youngauthoracademy.com

ISBN: 9798351642741

Printed by Amazon Direct Publishing.

Cover Art Copyright ©2022 Martin Wojnowski

To Mum and Dad,

without their support,

this story would have never been

released to the public domain ;)

Solange Wojnowski

Contents

Solange Wojnowski

- Prologue -

The man was falling down the rocky wall of a canyon in the middle of a desert. He was screaming, knowing there was no way out and realising that no one would help... Everything seemed so vivid yet so fake at the same time.

Soon the sky blurred out... the sweat, the heartbeat, and the terror stopped. The man laid there, not moving in the slightest. His grey clothing blended with the rocks below.

The man was dead.

Solange Wojnowski

- Chapter 1 -

Samantha Bridges jolted upright in her bed. Another nightmare. Her heart was beating fast, she could hear it distinctly in her chest. It happened every night. Not the same, repeating nightmare, although Sam wished it was. Sometimes such vivid dreamy flashes also occurred during the day. The dreams clouded her mind; she wanted to break free from them although she knew she couldn't. Her nightmares were almost now just a part of her; blended with her body and spirit.

Sam read about dreams from books in the library at her school at Durham's St Greenville. It was a phenomenon that scientists could not explain; once you wake up you tend to forget the details in most of them, but Samantha remembered the details in her dreams very clearly. They seemed to be almost like memories – recollections of experiences she lived to remember.

Sam switched on her bedside lamp and checked the clock next to the light, the LED display showed 3:02am. She let herself fall back on her soft pillow and pulled the duvet up to her eyes, wrapping herself as if she was in a cocoon. She was afraid of falling asleep, afraid of what was to come next. Did she want to experience another lucid nightmare? She closed her eyes once again.

Darkness flooded her inner sanctum. Images of a dead man lying motionless on some rocks. His head grotesquely tilted back. Blank eyes. It was clear that his spine had snapped. Sam flinched and started to run away until she couldn't see him anymore, she looked up trying to find her way out. She was desperate to wake up. She desperately craved to be back to reality. Just then, her bedside light flickered, then shattered, smoke fuming from what once was a bulb. Darkness wrapped out her bedroom.

High above, Samantha saw massive birds soaring through the sky. Condors with bulging eyes, gleaming. They surrounded the dead body, ready for today's meal. Sam didn't look. This could NOT be real. She will wake up. She MUST wake up.

At this moment, she felt she was somewhere in South America. Peru perhaps?

She cried out. It was not possible, you can't feel pain in dreams or nightmares. A condor with talons that looked more like kitchen knives. It flew just above her head. It scraped her. She was afraid the giant bird would scoop her up lifting her and carrying her kilometres in the air. Sam screamed and didn't stop running. Her legs weakened.

Then the echo could be heard. Distant. Calm.

"Wake up Samantha! It's all ok, we are here for you."

A condor was now swooping down at her, aiming for her throat. Samantha gasped, panting, tears streaming down her cheeks. She barely managed to open her eyes. Her parents were standing next to her bed.

Her mum was cradling her in her arms. "It's ok darling."

She then heard one of them say, "You need to calm-" the rest of her sentence was suddenly blocked out. Her heart was still pounding furiously.

It was morning already. For breakfast she had waffles and french toast that her mother had prepared for her. She worked from home for some company which rarely allowed her holidays. Sam's mum had business meetings every month. She travelled extensively to many exotic countries. All trips had been arranged at the last minute. At a days notice.

Sam did not really know where her dad worked. He did not like to talk about it. It didn't really matter so much where he worked as he was rarely home. Sometimes she wondered if she really had a father. She often felt the feeling of helplessness that orphans must typically have felt.

Today it was a rare occasion when all the family was sitting together around the table. The kitchen had a wide tall window with a flower pot that sat on the ledge outside. Sam always remembered to water the plant so it didn't feel as lonely as Sam did.

It was her dad that broke the silence, "What was it today?"

He was addressing Samantha but was looking down at his hands, typing something on his iPad. Her dad's name was John. Her mother, Amanda, looked up glaring at him as if trying to warn or scold him.

Samantha did not like to talk about her nightmares. She kept them all to herself. All bottled up. Locked within her pounding heart. All the nightmares she ever had. Painfully vivid as if she was experiencing them herself. Suicide, murder, accidents, incidents. Innocent or guilty, she hated them all.

She looked her dad in the eye. "A man fell off some cliff," she said matter-of-factly. She noted how her dad's expression had changed. He nodded, lost deep in thought, laboriously typing.

As Sam finished her breakfast, she got up from the table and trotted up to her room. It was time to get prepared for school. Her uniform was a white dress that had a brick-red apron and she hated it. She would much rather wear trousers but she knew that she would get into trouble if she did, as uniforms were obligatory at St Greenville.

She went to the bathroom, brushed her teeth and combed her hair. She checked herself in the mirror. Sam had pale blue eyes and many freckles covering her rather small nose. Her hair was so blonde that it seemed almost white and it was always messy. She stared at her fourteen year old self with circles under her eyes that where still bloodshot. They made it look worse - her pale white skin - reflecting in the mirror.

Sam walked over to the front door and swung it open. It was a bright sunny day in Durham, a perfect ten minute walk to St Greenville. She said goodbye to her parents, forcing herself to sound jolly as she looked forward to the day ahead. She sincerely hoped that everything was going to be fine.

On the way, she stopped by Noah's house. They had been friends ever since they were six years old.

"Hey Sam!" he called out from an open window of his bedroom and ran down the steps to greet her. Upon seeing her up close, and noticed her dangling arms and tired face, he frowned. He was the only friend who knew about her nightmares.

"It's ok, Noah, it isn't real. None of it is, so please don't say anything. Don't concern yourself with any of it, I'll be fine!" Although Sam knew she wasn't really being truthful. The dream she experienced that morning actually left physical marks. The gash on her hip (the nasty condor) was gone, but Sam could still sense it under her skin. It must have sounded so silly to feel pain from a dream so she kept quiet about it and chose not to share it with Noah.

The first class of the day was Science; Biology.

"Take your seats everyone," Miss Wilson called out. She was an old and shrivelled lady. She looked as if she was about to crumble and the other students wondered how she still managed to walk, talk and be alert.

"Open your textbooks to page 313," she commanded.

Everyone reached down and picked up their books. Miss Wilson always had a croaky voice, putting effort into every word she articulated, but her eyes were glowing, filled with passion and enthusiasm a life-long, professional teaching career.

"We are learning about the brain," she paused, "deep inside the temporal lobe of the brain, the hippocampus has a central role in our ability to remember, imagine and dream. Our most vivid dreams are a remarkable replication of reality, combining disparate objects, actions and perceptions into a richly detailed hallucinatory experiences."

Suddenly, the phone on her desk rang so she picked it up. "Yes?" she croaked. "Yes, of course I will." She slammed the phone down, appearing apprehensive.

"Samantha, please gather your belongings and head down to the reception. Please do remember, I expect you to complete today's task." Her lips pierced together.

Noah gave Sam a reassuring glance and she knew that she could count on him to bring the notes over to her house after school. Sam smiled back, she felt comforted.

The receptionist, who was young and in her twenties, stood up as soon as Sam walked in. She seemed genuinely worried. "Samantha, I'm glad you came. It's your father..."

- Chapter 2 -

It was her mother who came to pick her up. They were on their way to the hospital, driving in their new Mini Cooper. None of them spoke a word. The silence was deafening. Not a whisper nor even a glance to one another.

Sam was leaning against the passenger's window. The rain must have started at some point. She didn't even realise when, and was focused watching the droplets of water hitting the windscreen. The wipers turned on automatically and were calmly swishing left to right. Right to left. Sam found it calming.

They soon arrived at the hospital; a rather gloom looking building. Samantha's mother proceeded through to the reception. The receptionist wearing a pale-cyan coat passed her, holding a slip of paper with the number 206 written clearly on it. Samantha guessed it was the room number that her dad was staying in.

She hated being there. The sounds of crying, and sick people; everyone seemed stressed and engaged, coping with their own grief situation. The lift was up the hallway. It was not pleasant walking up to it even though it seemed so close.

A kid then started to cry. Samantha looked inside one of the rooms and saw an eight year old child who was completely bald. She couldn't tell if it was a boy or a girl. She hurried on, ignoring everything around her, focusing the gaze on her shoes.

The second hallway looked identical to the first one. Nurses were rushing in and out of treatment rooms. People were comforting each other and saying that everything was going to be ok even if the doctor had said there was no hope. No one was smiling. It seemed all horrible to sensitive Sam.

Six doors later they had arrived. Sam's father was lying on a bed, asleep. The room seemed cosy, probably expensive compared to the other rooms. As they entered, Sam's heart sunk seeing her dad in a state like this. Helpless, weak, vulnerable, and at the mercy of the nurses and doctors' time and care. She did not quite understand though what was wrong yet.

"Samantha?" His eyes were now open. "Come here, sit next to me please?"

Sam sat down. She was holding in her tears as she knew it wouldn't help to show them. It wouldn't make her dad feel better. "What happened?" she whispered, hoping that everything was ok.

Her mother immediately cut in, not letting her father speak. "He was on his way to work. As he left the car, he turned around and was stabbed by some nasty mugger who was after dad's briefcase."

Sam looked down at her father. "Is this true?"

He nodded.

"Let me see the wound, please?" Sam insisted, but a nurse has just barged in.

"I need to speak to you," she addressed Amanda. "In private," she added, standing at the doorway, showing signs of impatience.

Her mum left with the nurse. Sam sat down on the bed and held her dad's hand. There were wires attached to his chest and a tube and needle in his wrist. She sensed her dad was going to be all right and he smiled at her and even managed a wink.

The experiences clouded Sam's head. How had this happened? She was so very much looking forward to the great day ahead and it is turning into a nightmare as if it was one of those creepy dreams. She decided she needed to find out what *really* happened to her dad. What her mum told her seemed like a lame explanation.

She knew enough about the weapons from the basic training her parents signed her up for. Yes, sounds quite unconventional but it's true! Whilst her classmates attended arts and crafts, football or spa trips, Sam was at the shooting range, studying different types of weapons and basic martial arts, mostly self-defence techniques such as krav-maga and tae-kwon-do.

It never occurred to her that after school activities were not typical for a kid (girl!) of her age. Her dad himself regularly practiced certain defence moves with Sam. It seemed suspicious that John got himself mugged so easily.

She crept towards the door and rested her ear against it. She heard a subdued conversation with fragmented sentences.

"....wound.....deep......liver......and......internal bleeding......so sorry." She overheard the nurse say.

Sam tried to hold back her tears. She was now feeling a mixture of sadness, anger and puzzlement. Something didn't quite add up here. Why were they not telling her the truth? She heard footsteps approaching so she immediately returned back to the bed. Her dad saw Sam's actions but kept quiet. Her mother then entered the room.

"What happened?" Sam screeched.

"He'll be fine!" Amanda replied and continued, "Our Johnny is a big boy and will pull though. Nurse says it was just a scratch!" A big smile illuminated mum's face.

Sam realised Amanda was a really bad actress. There was no point on probing her any further. They would not disclose the facts. Even though she knew that John's condition was serious, Sam felt strangely reassured. After all, she saw many scars on his body. Her dad always claimed they were childhood biking and rugby accidents. Now Sam wasn't so sure. She sensed her dad hadn't always disclosed the whole truth.

"I will sleep here tonight," Amanda announced.

"Do you have any homework?"

Sam thought about her Biology task. "Suppose I'll submit it next week," Sam murmured to herself. She turned to her mum and replied, "No homework whatsoever. I would pretty please love to stay here tonight. Right Dad?" she looked down at her dad who winked at her again with a vague smile on his dry, pale lips.

"Are you hungry, Johnny boy?" Amanda addressed Sam's dad and continued, "Sam and I are going to the café downstairs. Do you want us to fetch you something?"

Sam wasn't quite sure why Amanda was raising her voice, her dad's hearing was perfect. She glanced at John who simply raised his right hand (the cannula-free one) to show a thumbs-up signal.

After a quick lunch, Sam returned to her dad. She tried not to wander around the hospital much. The place was depressing. Amanda drove home to fetch a change of clothes, pyjamas and all the essentials in preparation for her overnight stay.

In the evening, the nurse brought a folding bed in for Sam. There was a spare bed which was where Amanda would spend her night. Sam's bed was uncomfy. Her legs were sticking out as the mattress was too short. It didn't really matter though as she was engulfed by immense tiredness. It didn't take long for her to fall asleep.

***

Samantha recognized this place, it was Abbey Road, Durham. There were leafless tress on both sides. It was early morning. What confused Sam the most was that the city seemed empty. Only strong gusts of wind made the old, mature trees sway in all directions. Then, around the corner, a lonely figure appeared. It was battling the wind, holding her shawl, struggling to prevent it from being snatched by the cheeky wind. She instantly recognised the figure as Miss Wilson. She looked pale, unwell and weak. Miss Wilson walked towards Sam.

"Miss Wilson!" Sam called out but the teacher passed by as if she walked through Sam. She ignored the girl and seemed not to have heard her at all.

Then it happened.

The science teacher clutched her chest and blacked out. She fell onto the ground squeezing her chest. Her scarf had flown away from her but she didn't object. She was in too much pain and needed help urgently. It must have been a heart attack. Sam screamed for help but to her dismay there was no one around. When Sam tried to pick Miss Wilson up, her hand went right through her body. There was nothing Samantha could do. The situation was tragically hopeless.

***

It was daylight and Samantha opened her eyes. She glanced in the direction of her dad. Amanda was sitting on John's bed. They were discussing something in quite an animated manner. John tried to rise in his bed but Amanda pushed him back down and hissed, "You've got to stay here for another day or two. I'm sorry, I must put my foot down. The mission has to be postponed. That's it! I'll discuss it with Steven."

Dad seemed much better today which was quite unbelievable if you think about the seriousness of his injury.

"Good morning!" both parents said in unison as they saw her staring at them. Both displaying fake smiles on their faces.

"Whatever!" Samantha murmured to herself. She knew they were keeping something from her but what really mattered was that John was making a speedy recovery.

A nurse walked in. She looked cheery and bright. Her brunette hair was wavy and somehow blowy even when there was no wind.

"Breakfast!" the nurse announced in a singing tone. It was a different lady. She was a Filipina and served porridge. Sam frowned.

"I'm not hungry," she replied, pushing it away.

"Of course you are dear." The nurse had now placed it on a tray in front of Sam and just left the room.

Samantha only realized how hungry she actually was when she had the first spoonful of the watery substance. In a matter of minutes, it was all gobbled up.

Mum announced in a tone that expected no objections, that she would take her to school. Sam dressed quickly as the class was to start in twenty five minutes.

Both of them proceeded down to Reception whilst Samantha was looking around the grey and blue tiling at the entrance. She gasped.

In the adjacent emergency room, she saw Miss Wilson. There were two doctors talking about a heart attack case on Abbey Road. Samantha was astonished. Was it her that had almost killed Miss Wilson or was it that she had predicted it?

The words echoed in her head. *Our most vivid dreams are a remarkable replication of reality...* she dreamt a replication of reality. But it was not hers. It was Miss Wilson's.

- Chapter 3 -

Miss Wilson had not shown up at school for the next few weeks. Samantha didn't dare share her dream experiences with her classmates nor even her own parents but one afternoon she decided to bring it up.

The clock was showing 4pm on the Saturday afternoon but it was already getting dark – low clouds floating over the cobblestone streets.

Dad had been home for the last two days and his mood was jovial. They were all sitting with cups of tea and biscuits in the living room.

"I had a dream," started Sam, "Miss Wilson was in it." Both of her parents looked at each other. They knew what she was about to say. "I saw her in the hospital," continued Sam, ignoring her parent's stare, "and in the dream, I felt as if it was all for real. The most creepy thing was, Miss Wilson walked right through me as if I was some ghost!"

Sam's dad smiled and tried to calm her down, "Don't think about it too much my dear muppet. Mum and I decided that a nice holiday would do all of us some good. Wouldn't you agree?"

Sam's face lit up but she knew it was still some time until the half term break.

She smiled. Her mum smiled. Her dad smiled.

Sam grabbed another biscuit (*knowing well mum was about to snatch it*) and they carried on playing Scrabble.

***

Caltanissetta - Sicily- Italy

The room was quite large. Possibly the size of a tennis court. There were no windows and the ceiling featured rows of blue fluorescent lights. Fixed on the the main wall was a massive screen. It featured satellite image of Sam's neighbourhood in Durham.

About a dozen people seemed to be preoccupied typing something and checking diagrams on their personal computers. A tall man in his fifties wearing a tailored blue suit, white shirt and blue tie was standing in front of the screen speaking on his mobile phone. An Englishman, his voice was calm and articulate as he spoke, "Hello John! How is everything going? How is Samantha?"

John replied, "Everything is going well. I'm sure it came to your attention that someone stole the briefcase. I suspect the culprit is working with James Colton. Regarding Samantha, she might be developing her powers faster than expected."

The man in the blue suit frowned. "John, we cannot afford the slightest turbulence. Please tell me there was nothing in the briefcase that could jeopardise this project."

John replied without hesitation, "Please don't concern yourself with this matter, Steven, I will assess and manage the damage, if there is any. Please advise on our approach to Sam's development."

Steven thought for a moment and then replied, "Bring her here. I would love to meet our star."

He pressed the *end-call* button on his mobile and looked at the screen contemplating his next course of actions.

***

John had always worried about Samantha, her dreams started at an early age. She would forget them as soon as she woke up, but now she remembered all of them. He only found out a month ago that whenever something gruesome happened, Samantha was physically there; like a ghost. He became really fond of her and gradually started referring to her in his mind as if she was his very own daughter.

He and Amanda were in their bedroom about to turn in for the night. He still experienced some slight pain but couldn't wait any longer. John grabbed Amanda's hand and said, "Look, we need to go to Palermo without delay. I spoke to Steven earlier and he insists on bringing Sam in. But first thing's first, we need to track down James Colton and recover the file."

Amanda didn't seem at all inclined to support this idea. "First, you need to get better. Listen, I can go on my own. We know how to find him. We know his number."

John sighed, "I'm coming with you ok? Don't argue, you know it's pointless. Don't forget who holds the higher rank here."

Amanda gave him one of those 'naughty kid' looks and kissed him on the cheek.

"Boys will be boys. You are right. I'm done arguing with you. How about we fly tomorrow night? I'll arrange the plane and sort out the gear."

They both made themselves comfy in their large bed. The TV was on and playing "*Spy Kids 1*". They looked at each other holding in a giggle. John made a silly face and addressed Amanda in accented English. He tried to sound Spanish but it sounded more like Arabic. "Goodnight Ingrid."

Amanda replied in better 'Spanish' than John, "Goodnight Gregorio Cortez!"

- Chapter 4 -

Their bags were already packed when Sam woke up. She hated the fact that she had to travel last minute. She was going to miss her friends. Noah will be worried and she will have no time to say goodbye to him. Her mum emailed a note to school that, *Sam would be absent for a week attending a family funeral overseas and that Sam will follow the classwork and submit homework regularly as required.*

Amanda ended the note.

The good news came at breakfast as her mum confirmed they'd be flying out at 3pm. It gave Sam enough time to meet with Noah to let him know that she would be away.

She felt gratitude. Her parents must have really cared about her as they decided to go on a break now rather than during the half term. Her school didn't take it too lightly of students taking holidays during term-time. The funeral seemed like a good excuse and nobody would argue.

Sam ran to Noah's house. His mum opened the door and said with a scolding tone, "Oh, hello Sam! Are you not at school?"

Sam realised that indeed, the school had already started and would end at 3pm. So she wouldn't get to see Noah.

"I just came to say good bye as will be travelling to Italy for a family funeral."

Noah's mum looked puzzled (she has always been up to date with local gossip but this must have escaped her). "Oh, I didn't know you had relatives in Italy. Somewhere sunny I hope."

Then last minute she corrected herself, "I'm really sorry about your loss. Who was it if I may ask?"

But Sam interrupted, "Yes, indeed, we've been all very saddened by the unexpected news. Could you please tell Noah I'll be back in a week's time! Bye!"

And with that she ran back home. Noah's mum's gaze followed Sam through the half closed door whilst muttering something to herself.

Sam felt somehow fresh and enthusiastic after sleeping well through the night. When their chauffeur driven car pulled up to the airport's departures entrance, she was surprised when they were whisked through Immigration, straight onto a private jet parked proudly away from the maddening crowd.

Sam seemed really confused. They always flew economy class. What was so urgent now and could they really afford such luxury?

Smiley stewardess' politely ushered them on board. The jet's interior featured eight very comfy leather armchairs.

She was somewhat taken aback when she saw a man sitting right in the back row. He barely acknowledged them. He just kept his focus on his mobile phone. The man looked like a boxer.

He wore a loose black suit, a white shirt and a black tie. Some heavy object seemed lodged under his jacket. Sam was shocked, '*It might have been a gun*.' She quickly dismissed the thought. They all took their seats. Sam could see that Amanda had also been alerted by the man's presence. The man's expression didn't change and Sam got *really* creeped out by him.

Half way through their flight, she could not control herself any longer. '*They say 'curiosity killed the cat', but I'm a human*' - the thought crossed her mind.

She went to the toilet, and having to pass by the man in black, she sensed her heartbeat rising. She *had* to find out who he was. The man was now wearing dark sunglasses. His head was slightly tilted to the right. Though he seemed to be submerged in thoughts looking through the porthole of a window, Sam sensed he was actually watching her. She couldn't tell as his glasses were so dark.

'Gosh!' Sam recalled the movie, "Men In Black." What if he was a secret agent protecting our planet from the alien forces?

On the way back from the washroom, she dared to take a seat right next to him. Amanda's disapproving glance from the front didn't prevent Sam from taking action.

"Hello!" she said in a shy manner, "my name is Sam. What's your name?"

Sam tried to look the man in his (invisible) eyes and then smiled, she felt her cheeks turning red.

The man turned his bold head towards Sam. He managed a vague grin.

Without taking his glasses off he answered, placing his right palm on his chest, "Faranda. Matteo Faranda." He then moved his hand away from his chest and made a gesture with his thumb and index finger closing together. He continued, "Umm, Un poco Inglese, uh, little English."

Sam didn't give up and felt more determined than ever to find out who he was and what he was doing on this plane. He seemed friendly enough. A friendly giant! She gathered her thoughts and blurted out, "What do you do for a living?"

Matteo didn't seem to understand. He took his glasses off, revealing a scar just under his left eye. "Che cosa?... What?"

Sam thought for a moment and then rephrased her question, "Job?"

She placed her hand on her chest and said, "Student. Etudiante... You?"

Matteo smiled, "Security."

Sam kept wondering what purpose he had being on the plane. She thought for a minute and asked, "Why plane?... You?"

Matteo answered immediately, "Security!" His smile was broader.

Sam went on in broken English, "I see, you security of the plane?"

Matteo placed both of his palms on his chest and replied, giggling, "Si, yes, security of the plane."

Sam really wanted to keep chatting with this friendly character but she noticed the stewardess pointing the seats. They were about to land. She raised from out of the seat and in this moment, Matteo reached out and grabbed her arm.

With his right arm, he passed her a business card and said, "Security, protection? Problem? No problem." He smiled at her, letting Sam go. He put his glasses back on and made himself comfy for the landing. He had been wearing a seatbelt throughout the duration of the flight.

Sam tried out her Italian, "Grazie mille. Thank you!"

Touchdown! They had landed.

The pilot announced, "Ladies and gentlemen, this is your captain speaking, we have arrived in Sicily, Italy with a local time of 7:00pm."

He then continued in Italian, "Signore e signori, parla il vostro capitano, siamo arrivati in Sicilia, in Italia. L'ora locale è 14:00."

Matteo Faranda seemed to have livened up. He waved his hand in a 'good bye' gesture to Sam.

Samantha reluctantly got up from her seat and gathered her belongings. John had helped her take the hand luggage out of the overhead compartment. As the three of them proceeded through to Passport Control, Samantha glanced out of the windows at the small private jet that she just arrived on, taking in the exotic scenery. She was bursting with excitement. This was her first trip to Italy.

A driver waited for them outside, calling their name in the rattle of noise. The honking and shouting was making Sam feel dizzy. Two cars had just collided and their drivers were getting out of their cars, raging at each other, showing all kinds of gestures that Sam wasn't familiar with. Behind them stood the airport of Palermo, a blue and orange building.

The words, 'Aeroporto Internazionale Di Palermo // Falcone e Borsellino' were written in capital letters above the main entrance.

They all clumped into the limo and were off. The driver was expertly navigating the narrow streets of Palermo occasionally murmuring, perhaps cursing something to himself in Italian.

Sam felt like giggling as the driver reminded her of Mr Gru, her favourite cartoon character.

Italy felt like a completely different world to Sam. Houses were stacked on top of each other cascading up the mountain and the sand coloured buildings by the coast seemed magical. As the sea glistened in the sunlight, boats docked across the landscape.

Sam tried to chat with her parents but both of them seemed somehow detached. The minute they left the plane they both plugged in their earphones, and were intently listening to something. They both seemed totally absorbed as if nothing else around them existed.

"Hello Neil," he chuckled a bit, *"meet me tomorrow, we have a matter on our hands. We can discuss it then..."* he paused. *"...no, someplace casual, where they least expect me to be... ModCafé, 9:00? Sure, yes, bye, see you there."*

At some point, they both stared at each other, nodding and took the earplugs off almost simultaneously. Sam's mum looked at her then at John and started to nod. "Isn't it a cool track, darling?"

John nodded approvingly.

The hotel was by the sea. It was five storeys high, each room with a small balcony. "We arrived at Rocco Forte Villa Igiea," the driver said.

Amanda tipped the driver and they all stepped out of the vehicle. The heat struck them almost immediately, blinding them. As they entered the gates, a bellboy took their luggage inside. The three were greeted by a literal castle looming over them. There was a turquoise, green dome on top of one of the pillars that made it look more like a cathedral than a hotel. The main colour of the building was beige and intricate details were carved into it. Samantha guessed it was historical. It looked a lot like *Hogwarts* to Sam.

The courtyard they were standing in had grey tiling that was arranged into squares. In the centre stood a small statue reaching up to Sam's neck. It represented a wave. It was made of silver and bronze and it had a white, marble base.

To the left, Sam noticed a huge, beige monument of a man holding a sword high above his head. The rest of the courtyard was surrounded by hedges and trees.

Sam gasped as the bell-boy lead them inside the stunning building. The decor was adorned with Velvet and Gold. It was all very opulent.

"How did you afford this?" Sam whispered to her mother.

She didn't reply.

They rented two joining rooms, one for Samantha and the other one for her parents. There was a queen size bed at the centre of the room with a gold headboard and an 85-inch TV facing the bed. To the left, there was a desk and an armchair. A window was wide open revealing a balustrade. To the right, a hallway leading to a walk-in closet and a massive bathroom, also decorated in gold. The shower cubicle could hold at least twenty people. It felt very luxurious although Sam thought it was actually quite kitsch.

Amanda turned to Sam, "How do you like it?"

Samantha turned suddenly, feeling startled.

"It's….nice," she replied. Evening arrived quickly.

Amanda continued, "Dad went down to dinner, I will go too, care to join?"

"I'm a bit tired, I think I'll have a nap. Am probably a little jet-lagged."

Samantha yawned. Her mother nodded and closed the door. She opened the door again saying, "Oh, by the way, mummy and daddy might have something to attend to tomorrow morning. There is this amazing farmer's market.

Apparently the gorgonzola is to die for. So... don't feel alarmed if we are slightly late for breakfast."

The bed covers where cosy. Sam had to force herself to get up and shut the window.

What came next was neither a nightmare nor a dream. Samantha couldn't remember if she had gone to bed or not. Her mind forced her to see something. A vision... what a weird feeling. The words 'ModCafé' passed through her mind. Then a building and a clock striking 9:00am. *'Weird!'* Sam thought once more.

She approached the bed, jumped in and pulled the cover all the way up. She fell asleep.

She found herself in a café, sitting at a corner table from which she had a perfect view of the interior. She looked around. She was on her own except for two other diners. She stared, astonished. Samantha was staring at her very own parents. Amanda and John.

Bang!

The shards of shattered glass blinded her parents. A bit of a flame following a small, arrow-shaped object. *A bullet!* It was flying in a slow motion, swirling. Then the second one came just after. Sam was bolted to her seat. Motionless. She was so shocked that she was unable to move. They were dead! Both of her parents slouched in their chairs. Lifeless.

Blood was leaking down both of their chests. Assassinated! Samantha ran outside the cafe. 'ModCafé!' She quickly spotted the sniper on a roof ledge of the opposite building.

- Chapter 5 -

It was still dark outside when Samantha opened her eyes. The irregular tapping on her window was growing in intensity. She felt groggy, presumably after the jet-lag and slowly and reluctantly she got up and approached the window. She pulled the heavy drapes away but couldn't see anything because of the darkness outside. Suddenly, she heard the tapping noise once more. It was coming from the upper corner of the glass. A small bat was repetitively bouncing of the window trying unsuccessfully to break into the room.

Thinking about her last dream, still vivid in her mind, she now looked at this helpless creature. Something that she learned during Miss Wilson's biology class struck her mind, as if Miss

Wilson was talking to her right now in a secret language. She recalled Miss Wilson's words, "Bats are mammals. The only mammals capable of flying. They symbolise death and rebirth. Sometimes they are known as 'the guardians of the night'. They are largely misunderstood and therefore, many of their symbolic meanings are inappropriately fear-based."

Sam pulled the chair away from the desk towards the window. She stepped on it and placed the palm of her hand on the glass pane where the bat was trying to break through.

Miraculously the bat stopped tapping. It spread its wings and called out. It was a high pitched shriek. Sam had the impression he looked into her eyes but she wasn't entirely sure. The bat quickly disappeared into the night's sky.

She left the chair by the window and returned to bed. The LED clock was showing 4.48am.

She grabbed a pad and a pencil from her bedside table and tried to focus and come up with the strategy for saving her parents' lives. There was no doubt her parents were in danger. It was not a question of 'if' but 'when' there would be an attempt on their lives. The dream clearly depicted the café (ModCafé) and time: 9:00am.

Although she didn't know what her parents' professions were, it never occurred to Sam that they might be involved in some form of dangerous activities.

Were they spies? Surely not. Mum? Dad? Not a chance. She sensed a rising terror within her heart. She felt confused. On one hand she was angry that they hadn't told her the whole truth, on other, she felt fear of becoming an orphan and growing up with some foster parents in a distant part of the country.

What about this trip? Were they lying to her? Did they bring her on their mission and actually endangering her life? Wasn't this supposed to be a family holiday?

"Wait! This actually explains it all. What they said in the hospital, private jet, fancy hotel and the spooky man in black. Was he some sort of a guard?" – confusing thoughts were gripping her head.

She was aware there was no one she could call for help. Only Sam, alone, must stop the foreseeable tragedy. She would have to seek the answers later.

Sam was twiddling the pen in her fingers, trying to figure out what she should do. Her parents were still sleeping in the room next door. She was fourteen years old and utterly helpless but she would not let that stop her. She was too weak and inexperienced to handle the assassin, plus, he had a gun. Acting alone was not an option. Maybe she could stop her parents from going out? No. It would seem too suspicious. She put the notepad down on her chest. Closed her eyes and concentrated.

***

Amanda was still sleeping. John woke her up and she jolted upright, immediately.

"It's time!" he said, "it's 4am."

"I'll get everything ready John." She sounded calm. "Coffee?"

Amanda opened her pink suitcase, revealing guide books, clothing, toiletries, sunscreen and her mascot pink elephant (*which she always took with her as her lucky charm*). All the typical kind of touristy belongings that would show her preparedness for a holiday (*should a custom official in the airport want to inspect her luggage*).

She emptied out the contents and the hidden compartment was revealed. Yes, it was a special suitcase designed in such a way that the secret pocket was never revealed on the airport X- Ray.

The pocket was accessible after pressing a 15-digit code. She typed it, '274774806875739'.

The lock snapped open and the secret pocket revealed: two pistols, one hand grenade, a flash bang, a tear gas canister, taser, etc. All the items one would need to complete the job.

They moved quietly to ensure that Sam wouldn't be woken up in the adjoining room. "We will recover the files, don't worry." Amanda glanced at John confidently. They put on comfy clothes and left the room.

***

The day Sam and her parents where in the limo on their way to the hotel, a man in his late thirties was standing in the living room of his penthouse staring at the sea view. His name was Neil Nastasi. His mobile phone vibrated on the glass dining table. He picked it up.

The incoming call was from his boss, James Colton. "Hello Boss, what makes you call me so early?" Neil waited and then continued, "Ok, how about same place as yesterday?"

Neil waited for Colton's answer and then concluded, "How about ModCafé at 9am?" Neil added, "Ok see you there, boss."

Neil was a local, Sicilian, although he wasn't brought up with the rich, he grew up in the poorest alley in Palermo. People still called it 'The Rat Den'. He felt proud to be more successful than any other member of his family thanks to James Colton. Unfortunately, none of his family members lived to see Neil succeed.

Neil knew at once what Colton *really* meant. They used a certain type of code. Whenever Colton mentioned the word "casually" it meant he was expecting Neil to meet him immediately at a park bench. Neil knew he had a new assignment.

He placed the handset back on the dining table, walked into the kitchen, picked up a glass, filled it up with tap water and returned to the living room window. He opened it with one hand and watered the blooming flowers (*all pink*) in the planter outside. He repeated the process with all of the windows. His flowers brought him joy. They were of all the colours you could think of. Neil was kind to the nature and he felt that nature was kind to him too.

He put his grey coat on. It was long reaching down to his ankles. He slipped his phone into the inside pocket, grabbed his keys and a piece of bread from the kitchen counter. Neil left his apartment and proceeded down the communal staircase. He walked confidently, leaving the building behind. There was no-one around and nobody seemed to have been following him.

A few blocks away from his apartment, there was a small park favoured by families, couples and dog walkers. He sat on the usual bench and threw some of the bread onto the pavement. Birds piled in, demolishing the food within seconds. He didn't have to wait for long.

James Colton, the richest man in Italy appeared out of nowhere. Neil was known for his moustache and sarcasm.

As soon as James appeared, Neil started making some remarks which James didn't find funny.

"Let's get it over with, alright Neil?" there was a smug look as Neil answered. They both watched the birds fighting over each bite. "No, I have all day, even when I die," mumbled Neil.

James Colton passed him two images, one of a man and the second of a woman. Their respective surnames were scribbled on two photo, *Amanda Bridges* and *John Bridges*.

"Same time?" Neil asked for confirmation.

Colton nodded. Stood up slowly. He looked left and right and disappeared, blending with the pedestrians.

***

- Chapter 6 -

Samantha was sitting on the passenger's seat of a red scooter, wearing an oversized silver helmet which kept tilting all the time (left to right. Right to left. Back and forth). She had trouble keeping it steady. Her arms were wrapped around the driver which was not an easy task as the driver's physique was huge.

The man was driving fast. He was wearing a black t-shirt and Adidas red tracksuit pants. His biceps were bulging and were covered with some scattered tattoos. His name was Matteo Faranda.

They were swerving between all sorts of obstacles, spread on both sides of narrow streets of Palermo; passing by market stalls, merchants, pedestrians, cars and bikers. The noise was deafening. It was only 8:00am but the city was awake, buzzing with life. She kept wondering how soon they were going to reach their destination. Her mind was racing. She went over the events of the morning and the plan of how to tackle the assassin.

***

Early morning, lying motionlessly on her bed with a writing pad on her chest, Samantha suddenly had an idea. She immediately rummaged through her back-pack and pulled out a business card. It was black with white writing, printed on heavy paper. She studied it for a moment and discovering a mobile number, she reached out for a hotel phone next to her bed. She dialled the number. No answer. She tried once more. This time she heard Mr Faranda's voice, "Pronto!"

Samantha answered, "Ciao Matteo! It's me. Sam! I need you help!"

Matteo replied, "Ciao Sam!!! Stai bene?!" He sounded more serious now and he continued, "you, Ok? Problemo?!"

Sam continued, "Not OK! Come now. Hotel Rocco Forte Villa Igea. Per favore."

Matteo didn't hesitate, "Fifteen minutes, outside!"

Sam hung up, dressed and left the room quietly not to wake up her parents next door *(in the adjoining room)*.

She walked out of the hotel lobby slowly, not to raise any suspicions, pretending she was a tourist going for a walk. Matteo was already there, opposite the hotel entrance. He held one helmet in his large hand, the other was attached to the passenger seat. He looked at Sam worryingly. Sam got straight to the point. In the mix of simplified English and Italian, and through body language, she described the events that she believed were to occur and what needed to be done. She hoped Matteo would not ask any questions or think it was a prank. Luckily he didn't. He must have understood the danger that Sam was in from Sam's expression; how animated and stressed she was.

***

They parked the scooter outside ModCafé and proceeded through to the entrance of the building a few blocks away. This, she remembered clearly from her dream. She couldn't forget the killer's silhouette on the roof.

They crept to the building's main double door (*luckily it was unlocked*) where Sam led Matteo up the crumbling staircase and he took a pistol from the back of his track suit. The wallpaper was a worn out with pink with flowers imprinted onto it.

"This is it!" Sam whispered. She tried the handle but it was locked.

Matteo lifted his hand in a gesture to move out of the way. He stepped back and then with full force moved forward, kicking the door down.

They entered the room. There was a man inside whose face was plastered by the signs of surprise and frustration. Sam could tell he was about to lean out of the window to reach the roof with his sniper riffle strapped to his back. Just at this moment, she sensed a Deja vu. Had she seen his face before? She froze for a millisecond.

Matteo immediately jumped onto the killer, wrestling him down to the floor. The gun that Matteo held had been flung into the air.

Sam confidently ran and grabbed hold of it. She was sweating. She could not really believe what was happening. It was all going so fast. She automatically unlocked the gun and squeezed the trigger, aiming at the assassin.

Bang! Sam shot him in the leg.

Matteo was holding the assassin in a strangle lock. At this very moment, the killer took out a small knife from the strap attached to his trousers and stabbed Matteo in his thigh. Matteo cried out, releasing him. The assassin took advantage of the brief pause, and darted through the door, down the staircase.

Sam ran towards Matteo. Faranda who held his palm over his wound, wincing glanced at Sam. "Va tutto bene, all good. No problem."

The assassin had left a black backpack behind. Sam picked it up, opened it and spilled the contents on the tiled floor. Inside, there were pictures of her parents, a gun, and a phone. She turned to Matteo, who was standing behind her, "He left this behind," Sam whispered.

At this moment, they heard animated chatter in the corridor. The neighbours were agitated and curious as to what was going on. Matteo put all the items back in the bag and they rushed outside, passing the neighbours, ignoring their gazes. They proceeded to the scooter. Sam gasped and hid behind Matteo. She saw her parents entering ModCafé.

Matteo started the engine and said to Sam, "OK? We go hotel. I keep bag."

Sam wanted to protest at first but realised she had no choice. She simply nodded and off they went to Rocco Forte Villa Igea.

Once in the hotel, she ran to her room, had a quick shower, dried herself off, put her pyjama's on, closed the curtains and jumped back into bed.

- Chapter 7 -

As Matteo Faranda arrived at his house, he parked his scooter, and hung his helmet on the left handle of the bike. It was about 9:35 in the morning, his family was awake. He limped up the staircase to the first floor towards his front door (his wound was aching). He shoved his huge hand down the track suit pocket fetching his keys. He unlocked his front door and stepped inside the apartment.

A five-year-old girl came running up to him with open arms. She was screaming with joy. "Papa, Papa!"

Matteo smiled back and replied, "Ciao, Maya, Como estai?"

A twelve-year-old girl appeared from the corner of the door.

"Papa! Cos'è successo alla tua gamba. Andrà tutto bene? Vuoi un massaggio?" And she peered at his thigh.

"Va tutto bene tesoro," Matteo reassured her and went up to the dining room. He dropped the bag onto a table, walked up to his wife, Carolina, cuddled her and kissed her left cheek.

In Italian, they spoke, "What happened? You *always* get yourself into a mess, Matteo! Talk to me! That stupid security job you have! One day you will not come home at all, you know! Think about your children. Think about me!"

Carolina burst into an animated tone. She buried her face in Matteo's chest. She looked up at him, sulking and then gradually smiling as if the sun was breaking from the clouds. She grabbed a tea towel, wet it, and wrapped it around Matteo's leg.

He replied, "It's not as bad as it looks! Anyway, let me get to work. We'll talk later!"

Matteo was calm. He hugged his worried wife, picked up the backpack and walked over to the desk in his bedroom. Then proceeded through to the bathroom where he patched up the wound. He applied a fresh bandage and went back to his bedroom, shutting the door behind him.

He rummaged through the backpack's contents pulling out the assassin's phone. He turned it on noticing the need for a passcode, obviously.

Matteo pulled on the desk drawer to find an ultra-violet light. He switched it on and pointed it onto the handset. The process revealed the finger prints. He could now figure out the passcode. The finger prints were on the numbers: '6,2,8,0'. Matteo knew that the combination of the code could be either 6280, 0826, 8260 etc. There were too many combination possibilities but he had to try.

After several times, he got it right. The code was 2608. The phone revealed the home screen. He dived straight into the messages, one of the icons shown 'Boss'. Matteo clicked on it. As soon as he saw the messages, he gasped.

"That can't be!" Matteo muttered to himself in a state of shock.

***

Samantha woke up to the sounds of curtains being pulled apart. Both her parents were standing over her. Amanda, "Good morning sleepy head, it's 11:30am already! You have been asleep for a while!" Samantha rolled her eyes and muttered to herself, "Yeah right."

"Guess what?" Her dad said, "We are going to the Caltanissetta clinic. There are doctors who specialise in the brain, specifically the hippocampus. They can help you! There is a good chance they will find a solution to get rid of your nightmares."

Samantha sighed.

"I don't want to go." She had come to accept that her dreams *were* her reality, her uniqueness. They practically saved her parents' *lives*. She didn't *need* help! She also couldn't leave Matteo behind after all he had done for her. She needed to meet with him urgently, she was dying to learn the content of the assassin's mobile phone.

Sam didn't give up, "I am *not* going anywhere!"

Amanda and John just stared at each other.

"We thought you hated those nightmares? It doesn't matter what you want anyway because we came all the way here to Sicily to meet with the specialists at Caltanissetta!"

Samantha was forced to finally prepare herself for her departure. She wore light blue, straight, ripped jeans and a white shirt. They packed their bags and headed down the staircase.

Samantha sat on a comfy large armchair next to her dad as Amanda was checking them out of the hotel. As they were waiting, a friendly lady came up to them, "Hello guys! I hope you have had an enjoyable stay with us. My name is Monika and I'm the Hotel's Manager! It was really lovely to host you and I hope we'll see you again. Should you choose to visit us, please quote my name, we will make sure to satisfy your requirements," Sam smiled and thanked her, "Thank you so much Monika! We will do so! I'm Samantha! We are heading to Caltanissetta Clinic!!!"

Monika smiled, raising her eyebrows, "Nice, Caltanissetta is a lovely place!"

John ignored the conversation completely as he was focused reading a message on his mobile. His face was turning red.

A black limo with tinted windows was parked outside. Sam did not like this at all. It made her feel very uneasy.

Out of the front, came two men in dark suits. They were wearing sunglasses, even though it was not sunny; it was in fact cloudy and they both wore earpieces.

'*What are they trying to do?*' Sam thought to herself. She tried to turn around but John stopped her.

"I, I think I left something!" Sam said in a state of panic.

"We'll replace it once we get there," Amanda replied, smiling, returning from the front hotel desk.

One of the men grabbed her suitcase and backpack, whilst the other grabbed her arm.

"Wait! Stop!" Sam cried out.

"Don't worry, we will join you once we put our luggage in," John said reassuringly.

The man who grabbed Sam's arm shut the door. *Click.* The driver must have locked it! Sam suddenly got even more frightened. What was happening? At that very moment, the A/C turned on. Instead of cool air, she saw a thick, foggy mist. Sam shouted and banged on the window, separating her from the driver and front passenger.

"Let me out!" she cried, pulling the handle. She felt her body weaken.

Samantha then blacked out.

***

Caltanissetta

Steven Brown had never felt prouder. Project 'Vespertilio' (*Latin for 'bat'*) brought desirable results. It worked! He was sitting at his desk facing John.

"So, Samantha has arrived. Is she ready? I'm so sorry that we had to drug her."

John nodded doubtfully. He opened his mouth but then closed it slowly. After a while, he opened it again trying to say something but Steven raised his hand and said, "Could you please fill me in on what happened in Palermo this morning?"

John bit his lower lip and said, "We attempted to recover the USB holding the genome sequence and development process of Vespertilio. We know that James Colton was responsible."

Steven's face turned grey.

"Tell me you retrieved it?" Steven hissed.

John felt his heart sinking down into his stomach. "Negative. Our mission failed."

"Are you telling me he has the files?" Steven questioned.

John gulped. In his thirty year career with the military special ops, he had never even failed a single assignment.

"That's affirmative, Sir. John Colton is in possession of the Vespertilio files."

The silence in Steven's office was unbearable. John expected to die within seconds.

***

Samantha opened her eyes, she felt groggy. *Where was she? How did she get here?* The last thing she remembered was chatting with the hotel's manager. Sam tried to take in her surroundings. A bright, white windowless room. She was lying on a bed. Various cables and pipes were connecting her arms and chest to several machines. It reminded her of when her dad was in hospital. She tried to move but to no avail. She started to panic, wriggling around. Her brain wasn't processing it all properly.

Lying flat on her bed, she wasn't able to bend her body to see if she was actually strapped. But she was sure that she was tied to the bed. Just then, the door opened and two men and a lady walked in. The lady seemed to be in charge. She smiled and greeted Sam, "Hello Samantha? How are you feeling?"

Sam felt anger. She was in no mood to talk. Not to be nice. She barked, "Where am I? What am I doing here? Can I see my mum and dad?"

Dr. Adams, as she introduced herself, spoke in a soft calm voice, "Welcome to Caltanissetta Clinic. Our facility is world famous for helping people like you. We will make you feel better, safer and comfortable with yourself."

Sam didn't like what she saw or heard. She knew she had to run away somehow. What about her parents? Were they alright?

Suddenly, the door burst open and a short Asian man wearing glasses in large black frames barged into the room screaming, "Samantha – is it really you? They didn't let me see you. Can you believe it? We are finally reunited! I must tell you..."

He didn't manage to finish his sentence when the security guards tasered him and dragged him out of the room.

Dr Adams smiled at Sam and calmly said, "Sorry about that Samantha. This shouldn't have happened. We have different patients here. He must have been one of them. Anyway, we will begin tomorrow. For now, please take rest and sleep. I'll check on you later."

Before Sam had any time to object, two doctors who were standing there with Dr Adams moved towards Sam. One of them retrieved a needle, and the other held Sam in place. They injected a fluid into her arm, sending her into a deep sleep.

***

Whilst John contemplated his last minutes of life, Steven looked him in the eye and calmy said, "As I mentioned to you before, we could not afford any mishaps. We had to take certain precautions."

After a dramatic pause, Steven continued, "You see, the USB in your possession was in fact fake. It contained a virus and a tracker. Whoever plugs it in, we will be immediately notified. We suspected James Colton of foul play. We have a mole in Colton's company; Bio-Pharm Technologies Inc. Now we can only sit back, relax, open our popcorn and check the screen, in anticipation of seeing the red dot appear."

John was motionless. He looked Steven in the eye and nodded, "At your service, Sir!"

Steven stood. The meeting was over. John raised, shook Steven's hand, and then left the room.

- Chapter 8 -

Matteo Faranda was heading in the direction of Rocco Forte Villa Igea. The scooter's engine was roaring. He was gliding smoothly through the crowded streets. Finally, the hotel loomed over him. He parked the scooter, turning the engine off, and proceeded to walk inside. He went over to one of the receptionists and spoke in Italian, "Hello, can you please connect me with the room of Samantha! Samantha Bridges!?"

The receptionist looked confused. She looked at her monitor shaking her head.

"Sorry sir, we are not allowed to share any information about our guests. It's confidential. Would you like me to call my Manager?"

Matteo thought for a moment and then nodded.

A few minutes later, a lady with very short, brown-haired lady entered. "Hello, I'm Monika, the G.M., how may I help you?"

Matteo shook his head.

"Ciao, Umm Italian?"

Monika immediately replied in Italian, "Oh Sorry, how may I help you, sir?"

Matteo asked her, "Monika, do you have a 'Samantha' staying with you. She's about fourteen years old, with blonde hair."

Monika smiled and replied.

"Sorry, you just missed her. She and her family checked out yesterday. They went to Caltanissetta I think? Oh! Yes! Caltanissetta Clinic!"

Matteo sighed and thanked her. He left the Hotel, mounted his scooter and drove away.

***

James Colton was sitting behind his exquisite mahogany desk. Neil Nastasi was facing him across the antique piece of furniture. His hands were clasped together in front and he was hunched forward. Neil murmured something under his breath, looking worried. James was still hesitating weather to kill him or not. If yes, who should he contact to have this taken care of?

"Neil, tell me why I should not kill you?"

Neil looked up, "Sir…Boss. I will not fail you again. I can do anything you wish. I am the man you can trust. Always have been. We've known each other for over ten years. Since the early days of Bio-Pharm Technologies Inc., and what about the files that you wanted!? I went to Durham to retrieve them, and now you have all the info on Project Vespertilio. I messaged you straight away."

Colton sighed and spoke calmly, "Why didn't you use the code? You should've known that they might be screening my messages!"

After thirty seconds' silence, James continued, "Why did you fail to assassinate this annoying Bridges duo?"

Neil then replied in an animated tone. He was sweating profusely. "If it weren't for me, you would not have the files and you would not have known the details of the project. You wouldn't know who Samantha was and any idea of her location. I had tracked them all down and retrieved the USB. Give me one more chance, Boss!"

Colton raised his hand as if to calm Neil down. He proceeded, "Neil, I own you. Everything you have and who you are... it's all thanks to me. I made you. I dragged you from this Palermo sewer. I'm at liberty to do anything I want with you. If I decide that you are of no use to me - I can and will kill you!"

The silence was interrupted by Neil reaching for a tissue placed in a box on the desk. He wiped his forehead. James Colton made the final statement, "I have the final assignment for you.

You will take this..." saying that, Colton took a small box from his jacket pocket. Neil Nastasi recognised the USB he'd stolen from John Bridges.

"... and deliver it to the buyer in Peru. I will provide you with his details later. For now, take a break and pull yourself together, man."

He handed Neil a new phone. "You will receive the buyer's details on this phone... Don't misplace them! This is your last opportunity to make it good."

***

Amanda was sitting at a table in the canteen with John. She was told that she wasn't allowed to leave the facility.

"What's going on?" Amanda's rhetorical question was quickly answered by herself. "We come to Italy to retrieve the disc, stolen by Colton. We brought Samantha in. Fine! But why can't we see her? I'll be honest with you, I've grown rather attached to this girl. And why did they have to drug her? You've got us in quite a mess, hubby. You let the USB slip. You assumed James Colton will be in ModCafé and now we are both facing Steven's wrath!" she spoke fast, holding a mug of coffee in front of her.

"Let's begin with good news," John started and carried on. "The USB drive was a fake. There is a tracker, and yes! Steven suspects James Colton. He has just assigned us, or at least me, to get to the person who stole it. The thing is Amanda, as soon as the USB is plugged in, its location will be transmitted to us."

Amanda looked pale. "Are we sure that James Colton was behind it all?"

John nodded slowly. "You can't run away from the past."

Amanda stared in shock. "It was an accident! Colton was supposed to be in the car! Not her!"

John shook his head. "You killed her in cold blood, honey."

Annoyed, Amanda stood up from the table and left the cafeteria.

***

Neil left a while ago. James Colton was pleased. He could now focus on other matters. He called for the driver and was soon off to the airport.

His private jet was waiting to take him back to his office in Milan. As the limo sped by the markets and restaurants, parks and apartment buildings, Colton couldn't help thinking how much he despised all those common people. Poor, smelly and without any direction in life. They were all useless.

James' motto was, *Work hard for your money, and don't give any away*. He believed that it really applied to him. He cherished the fact that he was never begging for money. He actually worked hard. His life had meaning. He was developing products that help this planet become a better place. A thin smile appeared on his face at the thought of it all.

They arrived at the airport and the next thing he knew, he was climbing up the steps of his luxurious, private jet. They were soon soaring above cloud level. James Colton looked out holding his drink (*special vegetable and herbal formula*) and watched as the landscape changed far beneath him.

One hour later, they landed at the Milan Malpensa Airport. He was escorted out and led into another limo, heading for his office.

Bio-Pharm Technologies Inc. was James Colton's business. It was based in Milan. His private office was on the top floor of the giant skyscraper with his company name, 'Bio-Pharm Technologies Inc. HQ' illuminated on top. He asked his P.A. not to disturb him. He was now pacing around the room holding a photograph in his right hand. It depicted a lady with black hair and blue eyes. She was his long lost wife, Grace. She was assassinated in the back seat of their Rolls Royce. He wanted the revenge. He knew who did it and he would do everything in his power to have the killer eliminated.

First thing's first. He needed to speak with Martin Hall. He called his P.A. in, "Suzie, could you check what time it is, in Peru?"

Without waiting for an answer, he started checking the contracts printed for him, placed upon his desk. Bio-Pharm Technologies Inc. were about to supply the vaccines for the latest virus outbreak. All governments will crawl to his feet begging to secure supplies. Little did they know that it was one of his own labs which had leaked the monster.

He was giggling uncontrollably imagining the astronomical profits ahead for his dear self-made company.

Just then, Suzie stepped in. "Are you alright, Sir?"

James replied, "Never felt better..."

- Chapter 9 -

Samantha woke up to the sound of the door opening. It was Dr Adams. The memories started to flood back in. She was suddenly filled with hatred.

"How are you Samantha? How was your sleep?" Dr Adams asked her.

"You will let me out this instant! What are you going to do to me?" Samantha shouted back.

Dr Adams smiled and said, "No need to worry. By the way, you have a guest."

A man in a white lab coat entered the room, similar to the one Dr Adams was wearing.

He was not that old nor young. In his fifties? Sam wasn't sure.

"Hello Samantha, pleasure to meet you! Let me introduce myself. My name is Steven Brown. It came to our attention that you're experiencing troubling nightmares. Well, our team of specialists, led by Dr Adams, is here to help. She will be asking you different questions which you will answer truthfully."

Steven concluded with a forced smile on his lips.

Samantha barked out, "Please let me out of this room! I hate it in here, I just want to go outside! When will I go home? When can I see my parents?"

Steven smiled at her and then glanced at Dr Adams. "I strongly encourage you to trust us. We are your true friends. If you're feeling pressured somehow, just relax. Take some time off. We have cable TV here, I'm sure we can also arrange a PlayStation. You might also benefit from exploring our spa's grounds."

Samantha sighed but finally gave in. An idea popped up in her mind, "I keep on dreaming about people dying. That sort of thing."

Samantha already decided that she would keep quiet about the 'predictive' dreams. They would think she was crazy. She continued, "Once I dreamt about my science teacher having a heart attack."

Steven nodded, Dr Adams was quickly scribbling notes on her pad. Steven frowned and then spoke, "Yes, it must be scary dreaming about Miss Wilson's heart attack. But no need to worry. Anyway, I'll better be on my way. Lovely meeting you." Both, Steven and Dr Adams left the room.

Sam felt shocked. How did that man, who called himself Steven Brown, know the name of Samantha's science teacher? Something was not quite right here! She was going to find her way out asap!

***

Matteo had already said goodbye to his family. His excuse was, '*Work*'. A part of him felt crazy that he was doing this for some kid. "*No, she's not just a kid,*" he kept reminding himself.

He didn't want to believe the messages that he had seen, but it was in fact, reality! It explained everything, the assassination attempt, and Samantha's disappearance to Caltanissetta.

Matteo entered Caltanissetta. He was driving his blue Fiat; his head was almost touching the roof of the car. Caltanissetta Clinic was a government facility. Admittedly, he was wondering how he was going to get Samantha out. You couldn't just stroll inside. It was probably fenced off and constantly patrolled by armed guards.

"Anyway," Matteo thought to himself. "I will solve that problem later."

He was now surrounded by the countryside. There were many farms; cattle, sheep and goats littered, grazing the green and yellow fields.

A few people were walking around, picking ripe fruits and vegetables. Ten minutes later, a grey contemporary looking building emerged, although it seemed to be completely out of place. It looked like a massive grey stone slab, with fences curtained around it.

On top of the fencing, laid some barbed wire. The words 'Caltanissetta Clinic' were mounted on top on the building. Around the fence there were warning signs like, *'Do not enter without authorisation!'*

Matteo gasped at the sight of the breathtakingly sterile structure. There was no way through without anyone noticing. There were four watch towers with armed guards sitting in each of them.

Matteo parked the car on the side of the road. His face was buried in his hands. Had he come all the way here for nothing? He would sort it out in the morning. He took out his phone and searched, *'Motel near me'*. He drove away, leaving the facility behind him.

***

Dr Adams helped Samantha out of the bed and disconnected the wires attached to her. Sam tried to steady herself, she had spent so long on that bed. Dr Adams grabbed Sam's hand and they left the room together.

"You are only allowed in the courtyard and the indoor lounge," she said and pointed to the two places. Sam nodded. Dr Adams continued, "I have to go see another patient. Have fun!"

As she left, Sam sighed. Now she could finally explore the facility and possibly get some answers. The two rooms were in an enclosed area. She wandered into the courtyard. There were massive fences all around, covered with barbed wire. Whoever these people were did not want her to leave.

As Samantha walked back to the corridor, she saw a familiar figure. He pushed her into the lounge, closing the door behind him.

"Samantha!" he whispered loudly.

It was the Asian man that barged into her room the previous day. The one who got tasered. He continued, animated, "My name is Dr Chang, I shouldn't be here! They are looking for me!"

Samantha was so confused. Dr Chang placed his hand on her shoulders. He adjusted his heavy glasses and continued, "I have not seen you for such a long time Samantha. You were just a little girl, now you are so tall."

Samantha spoke, "I don't understand. Who are you exactly?"

Dr Chang stood up, "I am your father!"

Now this puzzled Sam who replied, shaking his hands off her shoulders, "I'm not Asian! I'm from Durham."

Dr Chang shook his head. "You don't know! Of course... They did not tell you... Listen, we haven't got much time!" he looked her straight in her eye.

There were footsteps in the distance. He continued undisturbed, "I am your *God*, Samantha! If it weren't for me, you would not be here! You are my biggest achievement!

I can't believe I'm actually talking to you. We barely have any time left! You are in grave danger, because of who you are Samantha! You are very powerful... because of the development of your hippocampus. You can also control what happens in your second reality-"

Samantha interrupted him, "I don't understand! My parents are John and Amanda!"

Dr Chang shook his head and said, "They are not! I am! They work for the Secret Service. You cannot trust anyone ok! You have to run away!"

He placed a key card in Sam's hand.

"Now, listen carefully... Don't deny who you are! Know that you are special because you are-" His passionate speech was suddenly cut off. The door burst open and several guards ran in.

"RUN SAMANTHA! RUN! GET AWAY FROM HERE!"

A guard abruptly tasered him. Samantha knew that Dr Chang was dead. His body went into a convulsions. He had just experienced a heart attack, she was sure of it.

Samantha did not hesitate a moment longer. She ran out of the room, using the key card that Dr Chang had just handed her. She darted through the doors. There was a green LED sign above Sam. It read 'EXIT'. She followed the path, opening the door and into the open air.

***

Matteo was in his car. He had slept the night at the motel and was now watching the facility closely. A figure appeared, darting out of the entrance, through the gate. The figure was wearing a white gown with blue stars. He recognised her almost immediately.

It was Samantha!

He changed the gear to 'drive' and raced towards her. "Samantha! Here!"

Sam looked up with a worried face and rushed into the back seat, not saying a thing. They drove away, leaving everything behind them.

***

"Do sit down, will you?" said Steven pointing two leather chairs across from his desk. As John and Amanda sat down, Steven continued, "Samantha has managed to somehow escape from the facility. We will apprehend her and when we do so, she will be brought back. She will enjoy our hospitality indefinitely."

Amanda tried to protest. Steven raised his right hand," "Please do allow me to finish... As you both know, this facility is financed by private donors, various governments and NATO. A lot of resources have been poured into diverse research. One of our projects called 'Vespertilio' has brought astounding results. We believe that Samantha is the first human created entirely using lab-based genome sequencing. She is practically non-human. Or *'transhuman'* as some of the doctors here refer to her. We've focused on development, or rather, improving her *hippocampus*. She is capable of predicting various events. In most cases, her dreams point to specific persons or locations. In others, the projected events indicate places unfamiliar to her."

He took a sip of water and continued, "Since your partial retirement from the Secret Intelligence Services, your job was to act as her parents, monitor her and report back any problems. The key objective of keeping Sam, or rather, *Subject CB1-X001,* was to see how she responds, being surrounded by normal people. Our focus was her interaction with peers. Noah, your neighbour, was planted by us. He is a normal boy, human like us. His parents work for the Service. He's been tasked to be her *'guardian angel'* so to speak. Obviously, we couldn't tell him who Sam *really* was. Anyway, what I'm trying to say, is you will not return to Durham."

John and Amanda looked at each other as Steven continued, "New threats have emerged. It turns out James Colton is expressing an unhealthy interest in our research. When he stole the chip, we had no doubt he would embark on similar research such as Project 'Vespertilio'... This is not the case. It turns out that he has a Partner or an Associate of sorts. We are yet to establish who this person is. This individual, or organisation, communicates with Colton via somebody called Martin Hall. He is our key person of interest as he has the stolen USB. Yes, it has been activated and the location points to Peru."

John and Amanda were staring at Steven holding their breath. As highly trained operatives, they've already wiped out the past and were expecting new orders.

Steven concluded, "Your new assignment will be to travel to Peru, track down Martin Hall and see who he leads us to. Any questions?"

John started first, "What about Sam?"

Steven calmed him down, "Don't concern yourself with Subject CB1-X001. Once we find her, we'll bring her here. This is her home after all!"

Amanda sounded more practical, "We left our personal belongings in Durham-"

Steven interrupted, "The contents of your house have been removed. They are on their way to Palermo."

- Chapter 10 -

Neil had finally reached the Jorge Chavez International Airport in Lima. The commercial airplane landed after nearly a one-hour delay. He walked through the terminal building to Passport Control, wondering if James Colton had really intended to kill him. He was not ready to find out.

It has been arranged that someone called Antonio Rodriguez would pick him up from the airport and take him to Plaza De Armas. He would then be collected by another driver who would transport him to Martin Hall.

When he saw the short chubby man holding an A4 piece of paper with Neil's name printed, albeit upside down on it, he chuckled. He assumed this character to be Antonio Rodrigues.

He looked just like Danny DeVito from 'Matilda'. The comparison made Neil smile. Antonio smiled back at Neil and shouted, "Hola, Neil! It's me. Antonio. Welcome to Lima, Peru!" His face seemed to be getting red from all the efforts put into being heard above the hustle and bustle.

Neil shook Antonio's hand; which were weak and sweaty. He suddenly felt an urge to wash his hands. There was no time for the washroom as Antonio was leading him through the crowded Arrivals hall and into the car park. Antonio walked fast but seemed to be limping.

Where did Colton find this guy?' Neil began to sense a growing unease.

***

Samantha didn't know where they were heading. She was still panting uncontrollably. Who was Dr Chang? What did he mean? What happens next?

She was staring down at Dr Chang's access card which he passed on to her before being tasered.

Matteo spoke, "You will come with me. You will stay with us. You will disappear. It's what's best for you."

Samantha sighed. At this moment, Matteo was like a family to her. She didn't know when she would see Amanda and John again, if ever. She missed them but she refused to refer to them as her parents any longer. Matteo's Fiat speedily crossed through towns and villages, leaving Caltanissetta behind.

***

Neil was standing in the middle of the square waiting for further instructions. There was a black fountain in the centre. A green Jeep pulled up in front of him. The driver invited him in, "Neil. We will bring you to Martin. Get in," Neil nodded and proceeded as instructed.

After a three hour drive, Neil really wanted to get it over with. So many conflicting thoughts were bombarding his jet-lagged head. He regretted drinking all this wine. His head felt heavy. He was struggling to keep awake.

The car suddenly stopped right next to a red jeep. The driver and Neil exited their car but kept kept the engine running. Neil inspected the surroundings. They were in the middle of nowhere; on top of a massive canyon. The red Jeep's driver and a front passenger carrying a laptop and a small briefcase, left their car too. They gathered around the green jeep.

The passenger of the red Jeep introduced himself, "Martin Hall!" They shook hands whilst the other guy with the laptop set it up on the jeep's boot.

"Hello Martin!" Neil replied. "I have your package. Do you have mine?" The *'laptop man'* opened the smaller briefcase. It was filled with diamonds. Neil reached out to his luggage and handed the USB over to Martin.

Martin passed the USB to the *'laptop man'* who immediately inserted it into the port. Suddenly, a figure appeared seemingly out of nowhere. Shots were fired. Neil felt an impact of a bland object on the back of his head. He was conscious but dizzy and nauseous. He then fell to his knees. The next thing he knew, someone was dragging him on top of the cliff. Objecting felt senseless as his enemy seemed to have had almost supernatural strength.

Neil Nastasi was falling down the rocky wall of a canyon in the middle of a desert. He was screaming, knowing there was no way out and realizing that no one would help... Everything seemed so vivid yet so fake at the same time.

Soon the sky blurred out... The sweat, the heartbeat, and the terror stopped. Neil laid there, not moving in the slightest. His grey clothing blended with the rocks below.

Neil Nastasi was dead.

- The End -

About the Author

Solange Wojnowski

Born in the UAE, Solange Wojnowski is a passionate, British Dubai-based young Author. At thirteen years old, Solange is an avid reader and writer and has been writing short stories since the age of eight.

Solange has always been fascinated by mystery and drama. She has been researching the plot of this novel for around a year.

Solange's enthusiasm shines through her writing and learning, and her creativity and imagination is revealed so eloquently through her adventure-based short novel.

Follow Solange's publishing journey here,
www.youngauthoracademy.com/solange

or

[please scan with your device's camera]